The Honeyguide Bird

Patricia Sealey

Illustrated by Liz Roberts

One day Lesang and Dudu were walking home from school.
A brown bird flew over their heads.
'Look at that bird,' Dudu said.

The bird sat in a tree and began to sing.
'It's a honeyguide bird,' Lesang said.
He got a stick and hit the tree.

The bird flew away.
'Come on,' said Lesang. 'Let's follow the bird. It will take us to some honey.'

Lesang and Dudu followed the bird.
The bird flew to another tree.
There was a hole in the tree.
Bees buzzed near it.

Lesang put his sock on his hand.
Then he put his hand into the hole.
He pulled out a comb of honey.

Lesang and Dudu ran away with the honeycomb.
The children ate the honey.

The bird started singing.
'The bird wants some honey,'
Dudu said.
'He can get it from the tree
himself,' Lesang laughed.

The next day Lesang and Dudu saw the honeyguide bird again.
It was sitting in a tree.
Lesang got a stick and hit the tree.

The bird flew away.
The children followed.
It flew to the top of a big tree.

Lesang climbed the tree.
'Look out!' Dudu shouted.
There was a snake in the tree.
It was asleep.

Lesang quickly climbed down the tree.
The children ran away.

The bird followed them.
It was singing.
'It is laughing at us,' Dudu said.

Dudu and Lesang sat on a rock.
The bird flew away.
'We must give the honeyguide bird some honey,' Dudu said.
'Yes we must,' Lesang said.

The next day the bird took Lesang and Dudu to some more honey. This time Lesang gave some honey to the bird.
'Now the bird is happy too,' he said.

Activity

Look at this tree. Five things from the story are hiding in it. Can you find them?